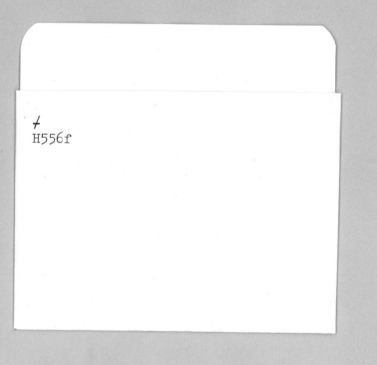

H556f

Fletcher and the Great Big Dog

Jane Kopper Hilleary

Illustrated by Richard Brown

Houghton Mifflin Company   Boston 1988

Big Wheelers—Justin, Lisa, and Pete,
and, of course, Genevieve, the big red dog
JKH

To Tawny and Tanya—and for anyone who has
ever been "found" by a "lost" dog.
RB

Library of Congress Cataloging-in-Publication Data

Hilleary, Jane Kopper.
  Fletcher and the great big dog.

  Summary: Trying to run away from a strange dog,
Fletcher becomes lost.
  [1. Dogs—Fiction. 2. Lost children—Fiction]
I. Brown, Richard, 1941–   ill. II. Title.
PZ7.H5577F1   1988   [E]   88-771
ISBN 0-395-46761-6

Text copyright © 1988 by Jane K. Hilleary
Illustrations copyright © 1988 by Richard Brown

Printed in the United States of America

Y 10 9 8 7 6 5 4 3 2 1

Fletcher was cruising along the sidewalk on his Big Wheel when he met a dog.

It was a big red dog with long ears and brown eyes. He stood in the middle of the sidewalk and looked at Fletcher.

Fletcher decided to cruise down the other way.

He turned his Big Wheel around and pedaled off.

He looked behind. The dog was following.

He pedaled faster and looked back again. The big dog was trotting along behind him.

Fletcher turned a corner.
The big red dog turned the corner.

Fletcher swerved into a driveway and cut across a lawn.

The big red dog swerved into the driveway and cut across the lawn.

Fletcher pedaled very, very fast. The big red dog followed very, very fast.

Fletcher shot up an alley and squeezed between two houses. He looked over his shoulder. The big red dog shot up the alley and squeezed between the two houses.

Fletcher did not recognize any of the houses around him. The trees that lined the street were different, and so were the cars.

And worst of all, black storm clouds rolled across the sky above him.

Fletcher wished he were home.

He started to pedal off, but too late! The big dog came toward him.

He sat very still and listened to his heart thump-thumping.

Out of the corner of his eye, he saw the dog coming near — so near Fletcher could feel the dog's warm breath on his cheek.

Thunder rumbled overhead and a gust of wind sent a flurry of leaves spinning around him.

He thought he might start to cry.

He looked into the face of the big red dog. The big red dog looked into his face. Before Fletcher could turn away, a pink tongue swiped across his cheek.

Fletcher wiped his face with his sleeve, and the big dog fanned the air with his tail.

Fletcher was beginning to feel much better.

"We're lost," he told the dog.

The red tail wagged harder.

"Come on. Let's try this way," Fletcher said, and he wheeled off up the street.

He looked back over his shoulder. The big dog was not following.

"Come on, let's go," he called.

But the big red dog just stood in the middle of the sidewalk and looked at him.

Fletcher shrugged. He turned his Big Wheel around and headed back toward the dog. The big dog trotted off up the street ahead of Fletcher. He looked behind.

Fletcher was pedaling hard to catch up. The big dog squeezed between two houses and shot down an alley. He looked over his shoulder. Fletcher squeezed between the two houses and shot down the alley.

It was starting to rain, and the dog trotted very fast.
Fletcher pedaled very fast behind him.

The big red dog cut across a lawn and swerved
down a driveway.

Fletcher cut across the lawn and swerved
down the driveway.

The big dog turned a corner.
Fletcher turned the corner.

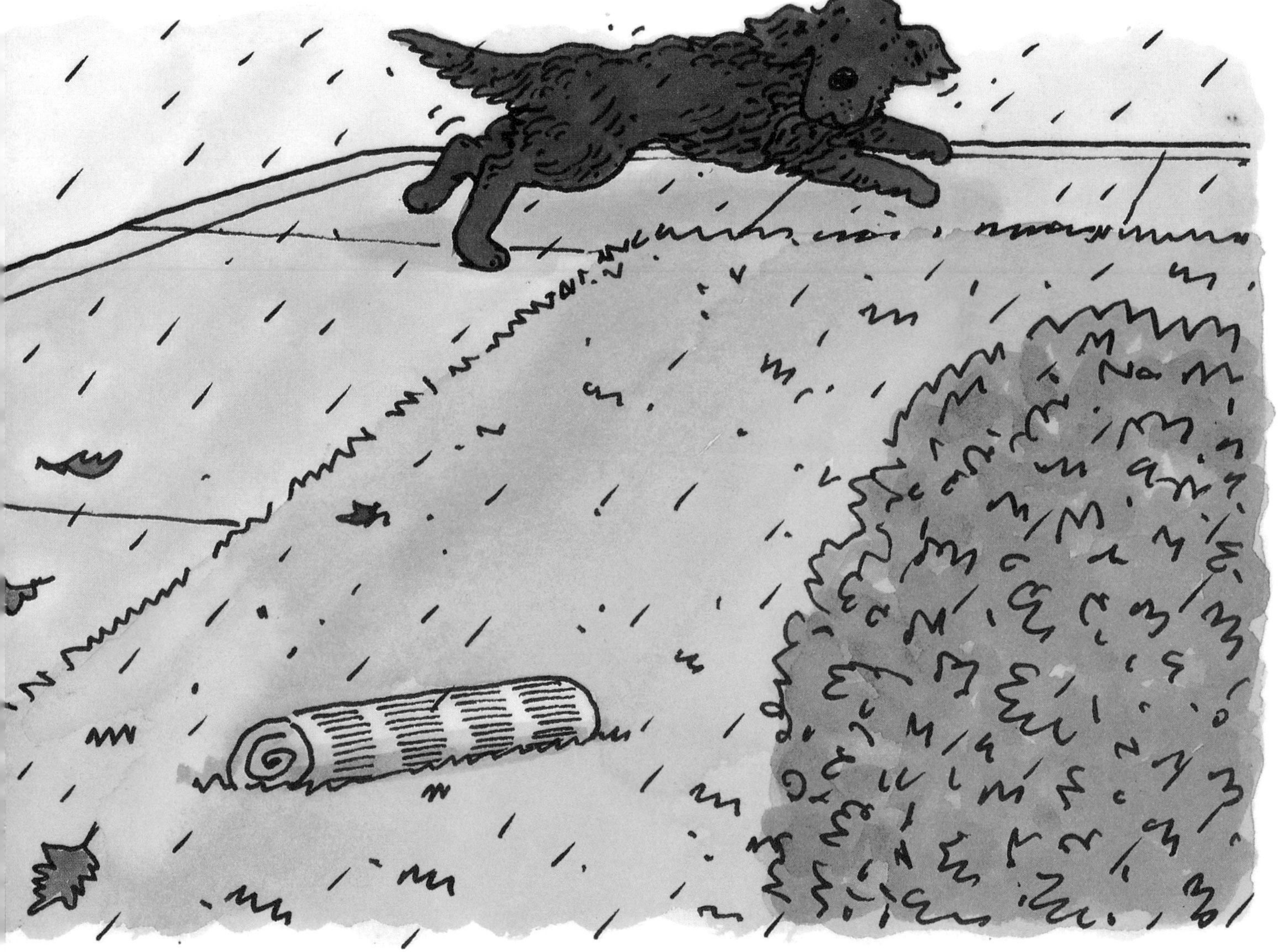

All at once everything looked familiar. They were back on Fletcher's own street. There was his house!

It was raining hard. His mother was waiting for them at the front door.

"He's my new friend," Fletcher told her.

"Bring your friend in where it's dry," she said. "I'll phone the animal shelter. Maybe someone has reported him missing."

Fletcher dried the big dog off with a fluffy bath towel.

He showed him his room,

and in the kitchen he shared a chocolate chip cookie with him.

At last his mother came in. "He belongs to the new neighbors around the corner. They've been looking for him," she said.

"Did you hear that?" Fletcher asked the big dog. "It means we're neighbors. I'll come and visit you!"

The big red tail thumped against the floor.

"Come on," Fletcher's mother said. "Let's walk him home."

Together they walked the big red dog home through the rain, holding an umbrella over him to keep him dry.